BUILT FOR SPEED
BOATS

IAN GRAHAM

RSVP
**RAINTREE
STECK-VAUGHN**
P U B L I S H E R S
A Steck-Vaughn Company

Austin, Texas

Published by Raintree Steck-Vaughn Publishers, an imprint of
Steck-Vaughn Company

Editors: Stephanie Bellwood, Kathy DeVico
Designer: Dave Goodman
Series design: Helen James
Illustrator: Tom Connell
Picture researcher: Diana Morris
Consultants: Lindsay Peacock, Ann Robinson

Library of Congress Cataloging-in-Publication Data
Graham, Ian, 1953–
     Boats/Ian Graham.
         p.   cm. — (Built for speed)
     Includes index.
     ISBN 0-8172-4221-X (hardcover)
     ISBN 0-8172-8071-5 (softcover)
         1. Motorboats — Juvenile literature.
     [1. Boats and boating.]   I. Title.   II. Series.
     VM150.G689   1999
     623.8 — dc21   97-48416
     CIP   AC
Printed in Hong Kong
Bound in the United States
1 2 3 4 5 6 7 8 9 0   02 01 00 99 98

Picture acknowledgments:
Allsport: 17t Stephen Munday. Banks Sails: 11b. J. Allan Cash: 18b, 22b. Craig Craft Marine
UK Ltd: 6t. FastShip Atlantic Inc: 29. Getty Images: 19 Warren Bolster, 23c & 24t Ambrose
Greenway, 26. DML Devonport: 13t. Amos Nachoum Photography: 28c. North News & Pictures
Newcastle: 16 Raoul Dixon. PPL: 7t Jamie Lawson-Johnston, 21t, 28b Mark Pepper. Quadrant
Picture Library: 14t Bryn Williams, 15t. Rex Features: 25 Sipa/Haley, 28t. Frank Spooner
Pictures: 21b Kermani/Liaison. Stena Line Ltd: 27c. Sunseeker International Ltd: 9t. TRH: 12b
Royal Navy. Wellcraft Marine: 10c.

Words in **bold** are explained in the glossary.

Contents

The Quest for Speed

As soon as a new form of transportation is invented, designers and engineers are busy trying to make it go faster. Fast boats have always had many advantages. When ships carried **cargo** to other countries in the past, the fastest ones arrived first and sold their goods for the best prices. Fast **ocean liners** have always been popular, as have racing boats of various kinds. Speed is an important characteristic for modern boats, and this book explains how and why the best new boats are built for speed.

◄ **Wind power**
The crew of a sailboat has to make sure the sails are always in the path of the wind. This will keep the boat moving along at the greatest possible speed.

▲ **"Flying" over the water**
A **hydrofoil** increases its speed by lifting its **hull** out of the water and "flying" along on underwater "wings."

4

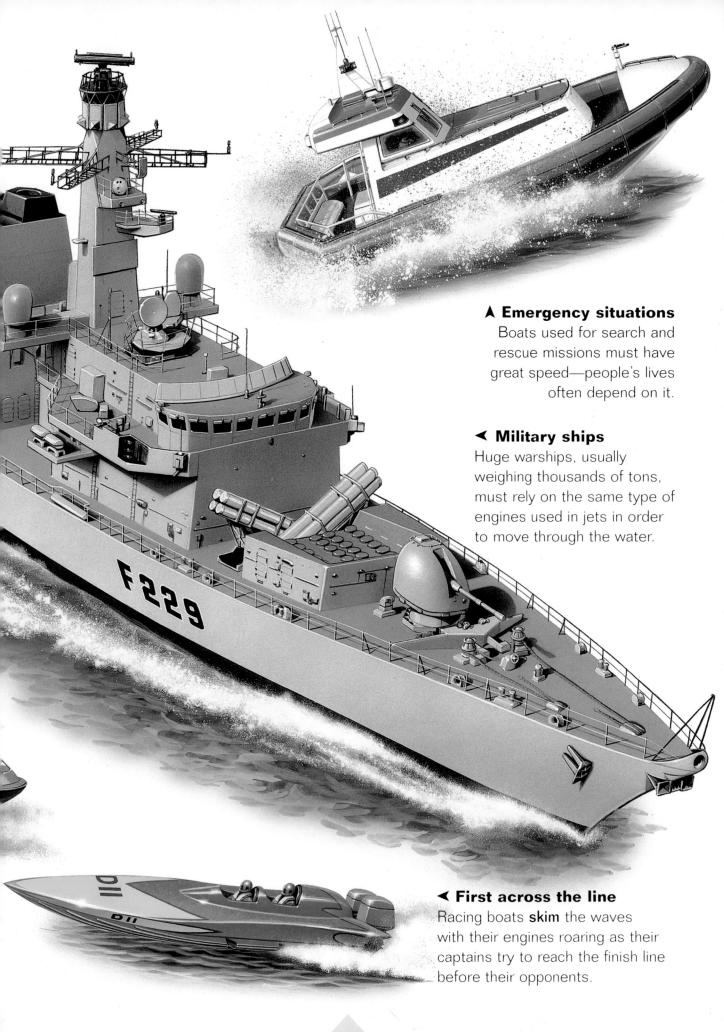

▲ Emergency situations
Boats used for search and rescue missions must have great speed—people's lives often depend on it.

◄ Military ships
Huge warships, usually weighing thousands of tons, must rely on the same type of engines used in jets in order to move through the water.

◄ First across the line
Racing boats **skim** the waves with their engines roaring as their captains try to reach the finish line before their opponents.

Designing for Speed

Designing a boat for speed means cutting out everything that might slow it down. The lighter a boat is, the faster it will travel. The shape of the hull is also key. The hull is what slices through the water as the boat moves. Designers make the hull **streamlined** so it will cut through water with as little **drag** as possible.

▲ Fun and fashionable

Boat designers sometimes get new ideas by studying other forms of transportation. This stylish little boat, for example, was designed to look like a sports car. It can travel at speeds of up to 50 mph (80 kph).

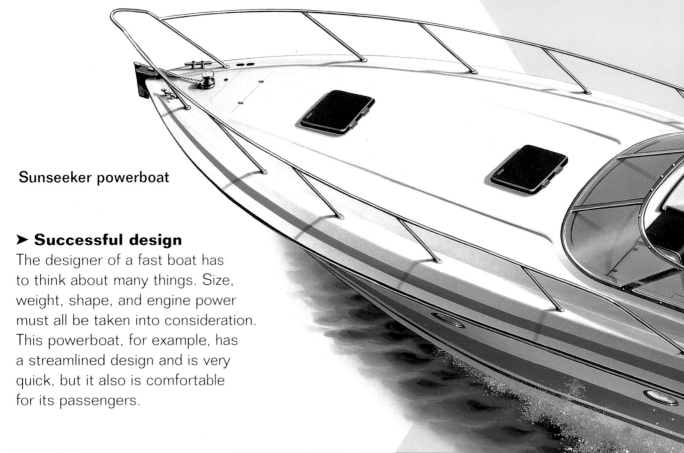

Sunseeker powerboat

➤ Successful design

The designer of a fast boat has to think about many things. Size, weight, shape, and engine power must all be taken into consideration. This powerboat, for example, has a streamlined design and is very quick, but it also is comfortable for its passengers.

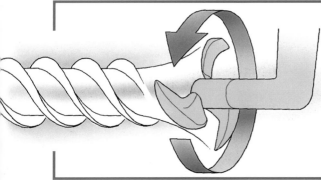

How a propeller works

A motor-driven boat has at least one propeller; some have two or more. A propeller has large blades that look like the blades on a fan. They spin around so quickly that they push water away. The power of this pushing moves the boat forward.

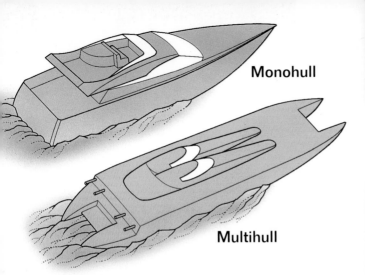

Monohull

Multihull

⋏ The fastest hulls

Fast boats are long and slim so they can cut through the water easily. Two thin hulls slip through the water even better than one hull. A boat with one hull is a **monohull**, and a boat with two hulls is a **multihull**, or a **catamaran**.

⋏ Paper boats

Some of the best racing **yachts** have hulls made from paper. The paper is made into a **honeycomb** shape, covered with waterproof material and then stuck to a layer of **carbon fiber**. This makes a strong but lightweight hull.

FAST FACTS

The speed of a boat is not always measured in miles or kilometers per hour. Sometimes it is measured in **knots**. One knot equals 1.15 mph (1.85 kph).

On the Drawing Board

A boat is difficult to design because no one can predict everything that will happen to it while it is in the water. The speed and direction of the wind and currents, for example, are always changing. A boat **pitches** and rolls when blown by the wind or rocked by a wave. Sails and engines also have a huge effect on a boat's movement.

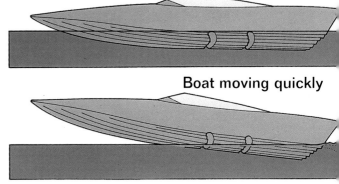

Boat moving slowly

Boat moving quickly

▲ Hull shapes

The hull of a powerboat is often shaped in steps or grooves. When the boat reaches a certain speed, the hull begins to lift out of the water, and air is sucked into the steps or grooves. This layer of air helps reduce drag.

➤ Luxury design

This powerboat was designed on a computer. It has a streamlined **bow** and a comfortable cabin with plenty of space.

◄ Spinnaker boost

A yacht can **boost** its speed by turning an enormous three-cornered sail, called a spinnaker, into the direction of the wind. It will balloon out like a parachute and force the wind to push the boat along.

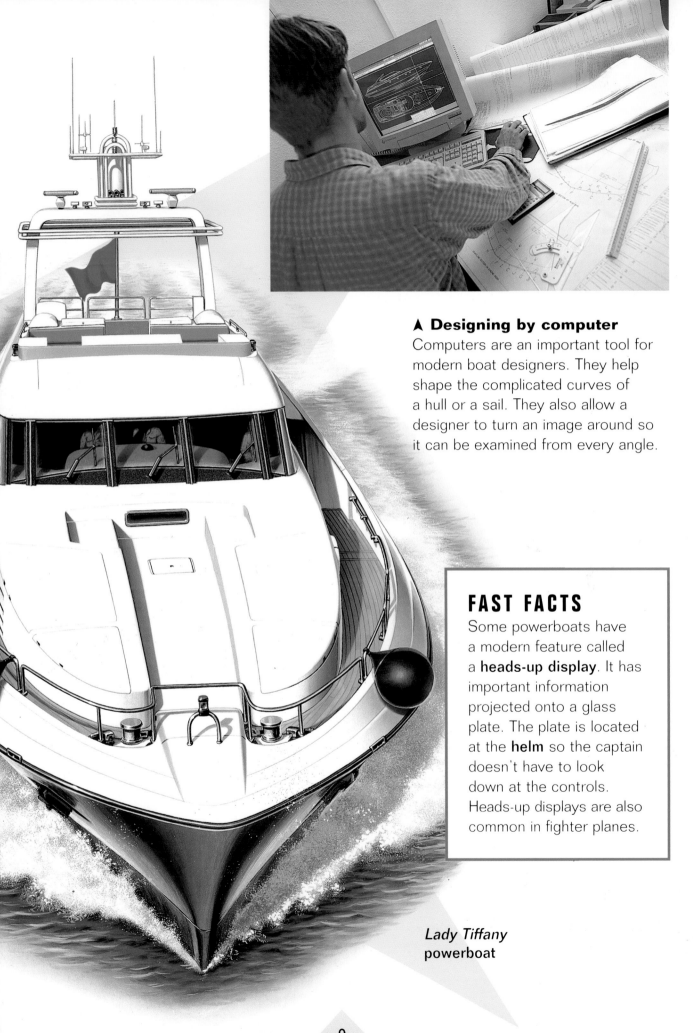

▲ Designing by computer

Computers are an important tool for modern boat designers. They help shape the complicated curves of a hull or a sail. They also allow a designer to turn an image around so it can be examined from every angle.

FAST FACTS

Some powerboats have a modern feature called a **heads-up display**. It has important information projected onto a glass plate. The plate is located at the **helm** so the captain doesn't have to look down at the controls. Heads-up displays are also common in fighter planes.

Lady Tiffany
powerboat

Will It Work?

A new boat is tested in many ways.
Sometimes a computer is used to
predict how it will perform before
it even goes in the water.
Sometimes little models
of the new boat are
placed in water
tanks. Eventually
a **prototype** is built
and tested at sea
or in a large lake.

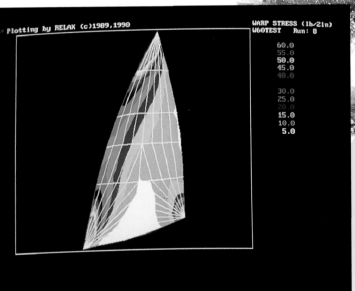

Plotting by RELAX (c)1989,1990

WARP STRESS (lb/2in)
W60TEST   Run: 8

```
60.0
55.0
50.0
45.0
40.0

30.0
25.0
20.0
15.0
10.0
 5.0
```

▲ Testing by computer

This computer is displaying the image of a
sail. The different colors show the varying
degrees of stress the sail will endure when
blown by the wind. The sail's designer will
make sure the sail is made of strong
material in the areas where the stress
will be greatest.

Tank testing

A model of a new boat is **towed** through
a tank of water under various conditions.
The model is then
linked to
a computer,
which records
information about
the model's
performance.

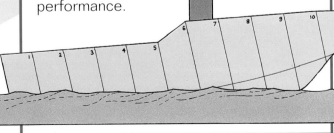

Inflatable boat

◄ Trial run
Different boats are tested in different ways. The hull of this **inflatable** boat, for example, is surrounded by a rubber tube filled with air. The testers have to make sure the rubber is strong enough to hold the air in under rough conditions.

carbon   polyester
foam   waterproof
                    coating
glass

➤ The perfect hull
A hull can crack if it is too hard. On the other hand, it will bend out of shape if it's too soft. Therefore, the ideal hull is made of both hard and soft materials. This way it is both tough and **flexible**.

◄ Sea trials
A new boat is tested during something called a **sea trial**. The specially trained crew make sure all the controls work correctly and study how the engine performs. If the boat passes all the tests, it can be put into service.

Engine Power

A wave runner

Many different engines are used to make boats go fast. Small racing boats often use gasoline engines that are very similar to car engines. Larger speedboats need bigger, more powerful engines, many of which are powered by diesel fuel. Warships are powered by the same kind of jet engines used by many airplanes. All these engines spin the propellers that drive the boat through the water.

▼ Jet power

Inside a jet engine, air and fuel burn together and produce hot gases, which then rush through a **turbine**. As the turbine spins, the propellers spin, too.

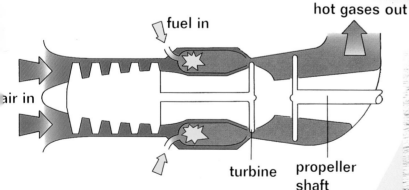

fuel in

hot gases out

air in

turbine

propeller shaft

➤ Nuclear engines

This huge submarine is powered by a **nuclear engine**. Nuclear engines are among the most powerful in the world and are used with only the largest military craft.

▲ Boats without propellers

This military **patrol boat** uses water-jet engines. Boats with water-jet engines can travel in shallow water because they don't have propellers. Propellers can cut into the seabed and slow a boat down.

◄ Wave runner

A wave runner is similar to a motorcycle on water. It is powered by a small water-jet engine, which pumps water out at high speeds.

An engine's position

A boat's engine can be located in a variety of places. Small racing boats have outboard engines that hang over the stern (the back) of the boat. Large racing boats have inboard engines, which are located inside the boat's hull. Some boats have an engine that is half in and half out of the boat. It is called a stern drive.

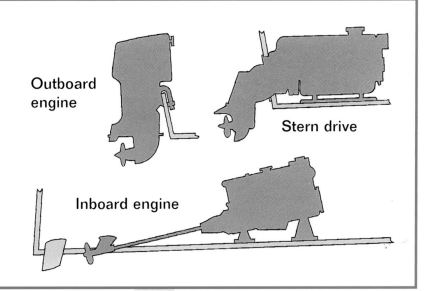

Outboard engine

Stern drive

Inboard engine

Super Racers

Powerboat racing is one of the most exciting sports in the world. The boats zoom along with their engines roaring, bouncing up and down as they leave tracks of foaming water. Powerboats usually race against boats of similar size, shape, and engine power. Races usually are held on huge lakes or in the ocean.

▲ Skimming along the surface
Hydroplanes are the fastest of all racing boats. They are specially designed to skim over the water and are often used by police and first-aid units. They can travel at speeds of over 124 mph (200 kph).

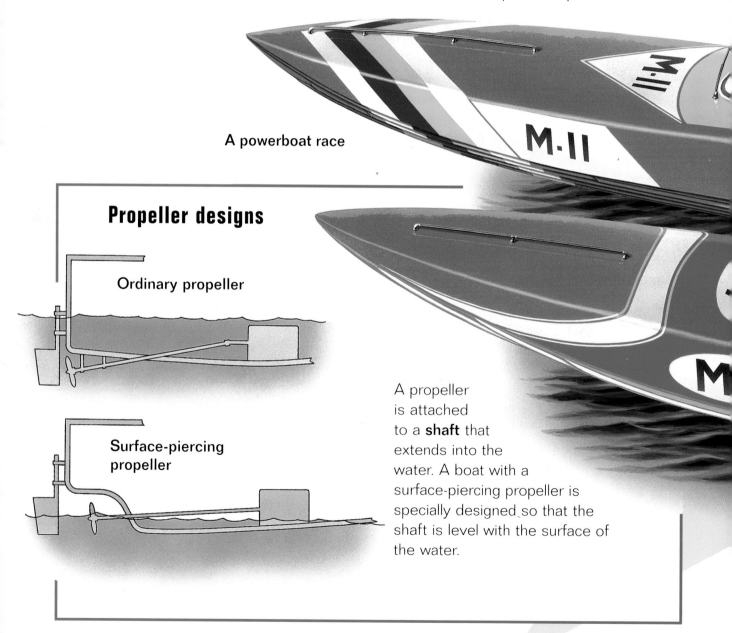

A powerboat race

Propeller designs

Ordinary propeller

Surface-piercing propeller

A propeller is attached to a **shaft** that extends into the water. A boat with a surface-piercing propeller is specially designed so that the shaft is level with the surface of the water.

▼ Racing cats

Many racing boats are catamarans. They don't rock from side to side as much as single-hulled boats. Because of this, they travel a lot faster.

▲ Streamlining for speed

A streamlined hull reduces drag. The top half of a boat is also specially shaped. The **cockpit** is kept low and curved in such a way that air will flow over it smoothly.

FAST FACTS

One of the most famous boat races is the American Power Boat Association Gold Cup race. Boats in this race can reach speeds of up to 150 mph (240 kph).

Across the Ocean

Before the airplane was invented, the only way to travel between Europe and America was by ocean liner. Liners often raced each other to see which could make the journey in the shortest time. Today fast powerboats compete in the same way.

▼ Record-breaker
In 1989 an American powerboat called the *Gentry Eagle* crossed the Atlantic Ocean in record time—2 days, 14 hours, and 7 minutes.

Gentry Eagle powerboat

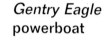

◄ Giant propellers
Any large oceangoing ship needs large propellers. This propeller, for example, belongs to a **tanker** that weighs about 110,000 tons (100,000 tonnes) and is used to transport oil.

◄ Racing clippers

The fastest cargo ships of the 19th century were called **clippers**. Modern yachts that are based on the old clipper design still race in long-distance events across the ocean.

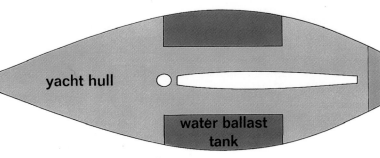

yacht hull

water ballast tank

▲ Water on board

Yachts carry extra weight called ballast to avoid capsizing (overturning). Water is commonly used. It is pumped into ballast tanks in the hull and can be released when the ocean is calm again.

Speed over the years

In the early 1800s, **paddle steamers** crossed the Atlantic Ocean in about 18 days. By the 1890s, the same journey took only 6 days, and in the 1970s the fastest liners could make the whole crossing in just 4 days.

1800   1890   1970

Under Sail

The best way to move early boats was to use sails. Now engines are a better way of powering boats, but people still enjoy using sailboats for fun or for racing. Designers of fast new yachts use modern technology to produce the maximum power from the wind.

◄ Racing over ice
Ice yachts run on blades and are the fastest crafts with sails. They **accelerate** faster than a Formula 1 race car.

▼ Sailing on dry land
Yachts don't have to sail on water. A sail can be attached to anything that moves. Sand yachts run on wheels at speeds as fast as 87 mph (140 kph) when the wind is strong.

A yacht race

Staying upright

The **keel** hangs down under the hull to keep the yacht from blowing over. Some keels have a simple shape, but other types, like the winged keel, are shaped to cut down on drag.

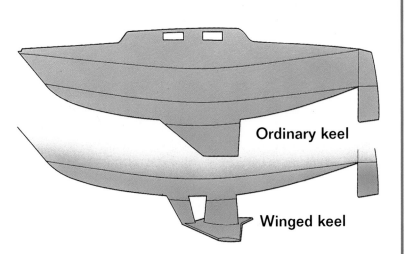

Ordinary keel

Winged keel

➤ Sailboarding

Sailboarding is one of the fastest ways to skim across water. The person on the board uses his or her body weight to keep the craft balanced and moves the **polyester** sail around to catch the wind.

FAST FACTS

The fastest sail-powered craft on water is the *Yellow Pages Endeavour*. This strange-looking boat has a tall, stiff sail and three tiny hulls. It is called a **trifoiler**, and it can sail along at 50 mph (86 kph).

Sea Cats

The fastest modern yachts and powerboats often have two hulls instead of one. These boats are called catamarans. The first catamarans were small yachts. Today designers also use the catamaran layout for big catamaran ferries. These ferries can cut through the water at very high speeds.

➤ Amazing sail

In 1988 the American catamaran *Stars and Stripes* won the famous **America's Cup** yacht racing trophy. The sail looked like an airplane wing standing on its end. This unusual new sail was controlled by computers.

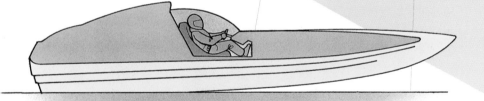

▲ Inside a racing boat

Luxury catamaran yachts have a large cabin in the space between the two hulls. Racing catamarans are different. Extra weight slows the boat down, so the crew is squeezed into a tiny space. Racing is not a comfortable sport!

▲ Fast ferries

The world's largest and fastest catamarans are SeaCat ferries. They travel at an average speed of 40 mph (70 kph), carrying as many as 450 passengers and 80 cars.

➤ Balancing the catamaran

A catamaran yacht crew keeps the boat from being blown over by using their body weight to balance the yacht. They move from one hull to the other as the wind changes direction. Sometimes they have to lean way out over the water.

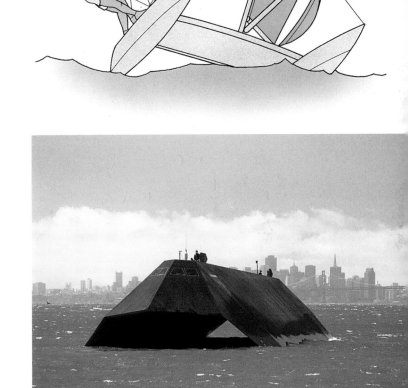

Stars and Stripes **catamaran**

▲ Invisible boats

This catamaran is a **stealth ship** called *Sea Shadow*. Its unusual shape keeps enemy **radar** from picking up signals that give away its position. This means that it can power along without being spotted.

Wings Under Water

A boat moves faster if its hull is lifted out of the water. A hydrofoil boat has underwater wings called foils. The foils are attached to the front and back of the hull by long stilts, or **struts**. When the hydrofoil moves, the underwater wings create lift in the same way as an aircraft wing. The hull lifts out of the water.

Boeing Jetfoil

➤ Special foils
The Boeing Jetfoil has flaps on the foils that move to control the flying height of the boat. The foils fold up when the water is too **shallow** for them to be used.

◀ Flying through the water
Hydrofoils are often used to carry passengers quickly and smoothly across lakes, bays, and sea channels. This passenger hydrofoil is a Greek boat called the *Flying Dolphin*.

22

Three types of hydrofoils

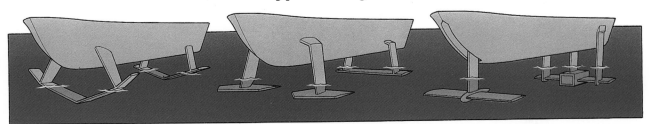

V-shaped foils

Submerged foils

Jetfoil

The underwater wings of hydrofoil boats are not always the same shape. V-shaped foils stick out of the water and help to keep the boat steady.

Submerged foils stay underwater and are moved to change the boat's flying height. A jetfoil has underwater wings and water jets to propel it.

➤ Staying level
Many hydrofoil ferries have V-shaped foils. The foils keep the boat level and make sure that it does not lift too much.

Direction of boat

Foil lifts.

Water flows around foil.

➤ Sea wings
A foil works the same way as an aircraft wing. As the foil cuts through the water, its curved shape means that it is sucked upward by the water flowing around it.

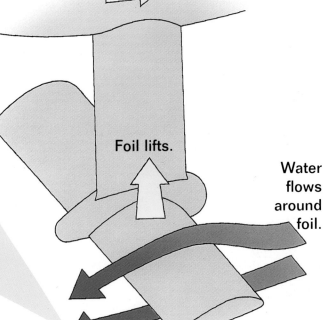

Skimming the Waves

A hovercraft is a boat that floats over land and water on top of a cushion of air. Big fans blow air into a rubber skirt under the boat. The boat is not slowed down by drag, which means that it is able to travel at very high speeds. The fastest hovercraft in the world belongs to the U.S. Navy. This boat can travel at 100 mph (164 kph).

▲ The largest hovercraft
The British SRN4 Mark 3 is the largest hovercraft in the world. It weighs 335 tons (305 tonnes) and carries 418 passengers and 60 cars across the English Channel. It travels at a speed of more than 75 mph (120 kph).

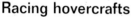
Racing hovercrafts

▼ Sports skimmers
The invention of the hovercraft led to the exciting new sport of hovercraft racing. Racing hovercrafts are small, one-person boats that speed along over land or water.

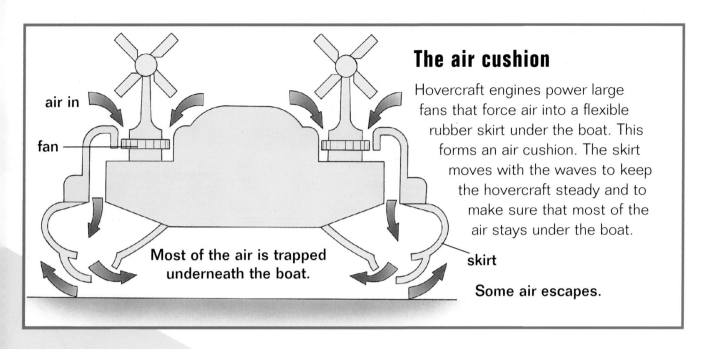

The air cushion

Hovercraft engines power large fans that force air into a flexible rubber skirt under the boat. This forms an air cushion. The skirt moves with the waves to keep the hovercraft steady and to make sure that most of the air stays under the boat.

air in

fan

Most of the air is trapped underneath the boat.

skirt

Some air escapes.

▼ Moving over land

Hovercrafts are useful because they can travel over land as well as water. Many hovercrafts are used by military forces to carry troops and equipment because they can come onto land to unload.

▼ Winged boat

Airfoil boats also have an air cushion. Short, wide wings on each side of the hull trap air underneath. This pushes the boat upward, until the hull rises out of the water. Airfoils can fly smoothly over water at more than 80 mph (130 kph).

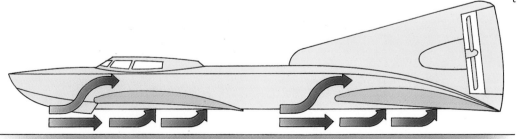

air trapped under wing

Record-Breakers

The official world water speed record is 320 mph (511.11 kph). It was set in 1978 by Kenneth Warby in a hydroplane called *Spirit of Australia* on the Blowering Dam Lake in Australia. He had also reached the even higher speed of 345 mph (555 kph) in test runs. As more powerful engines are developed and new hull designs are invented, faster and faster boats will be built.

Destriero powerboat

▲ Brilliant Bluebirds

The Englishman Donald Campbell set many speed records on land and water in his blue cars and boats, all called *Bluebird*. He was killed in 1967 while trying to beat his own water speed record of 275 mph (444 kph) in a *Bluebird* boat.

▶ Across the Atlantic Ocean

The record for the fastest Atlantic crossing is 2 days, 10 hours, and 35 minutes. It was set in 1992 by the powerboat *Destriero*.

➤ Fastest ocean liner

SS *United States* is the fastest passenger ship to cross the Atlantic Ocean. In 1952 it made the crossing in 3 days, 10 hours, and 40 minutes.

◄ Quick ferry

The Stena HSS (High-speed Sea Service) *Explorer* is the fastest car ferry in the world. Four water jets pump out 92 tons (84 tonnes) of water every second, giving the enormous ship a top speed of 50 mph (80 kph).

Around the world

The Whitbread Round-the-World Race is the oldest around-the-world yacht race. It began in 1973, and it is held every four years. The yachts take about nine months to sail more than 34,175 miles (55,000 km). The leading yachts often try to set new speed records during the race.

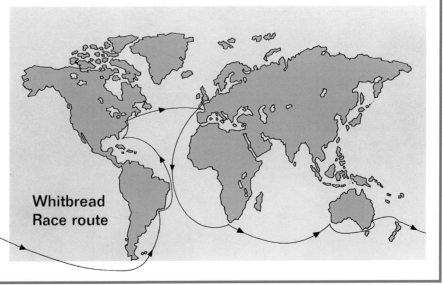

Whitbread Race route

Shaping the Future

Even after thousands of years of boat-building, designers are still thinking of new boat designs. Better materials and engines lead to new types of boats. Ideas that failed the first time around can be reworked using new technology such as computers. This means that there will always be ideas for new boats that can travel through or over water faster than ever before.

▼ Boat, or plane?

A new boat called a Sea Wing is designed to fly over the surface of the water. As it accelerates, its short wings trap a cushion of air underneath that lifts the craft out of the water. It will fly as fast as an aircraft.

▼ Aircraft wings

A **wingsail boat** has a sail that is solid, like an aircraft wing. This boat, called the *Walker Planesail*, has three tall, stiff wings that are moved by computer. The *Planesail* travels a lot faster than boats with cloth sails.

▲ Jet submarine

Deep Flight is a new type of submarine. Ordinary submarines control their depth by letting water in and out of **ballast** tanks. *Deep Flight* works more like a jet fighter. It uses its wings, tail, and **fins** to control its movements. It "flies" through the water.

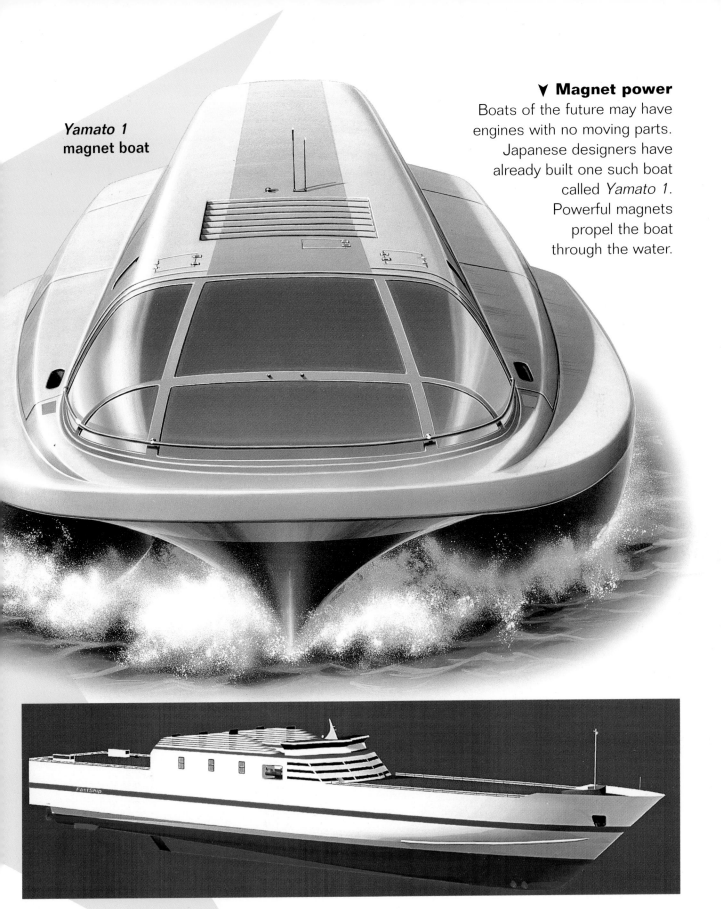

Yamato 1
magnet boat

▼ Magnet power

Boats of the future may have engines with no moving parts. Japanese designers have already built one such boat called *Yamato 1*. Powerful magnets propel the boat through the water.

▲ Extra-wide boat

A new U.S. boat design called FastShip is unusual because its **stern** is wide and hollow. Ordinary boats have a long, thin stern that sinks down in the water, but FastShip lifts up at the back. This allows it to travel faster.

Glossary

accelerate
To move faster and faster.

America's Cup
The most famous yacht-racing trophy in the world. Crews from many different countries take part. There are seven races in the competition, and the yacht that wins the most races is the overall winner.

ballast
Extra weight carried by light boats such as yachts. This weight keeps the boat steady in the water. Ballast can be anything heavy, such as iron, lead, concrete, or water.

boost
To increase speed by adding extra fuel or power.

bow
The front of a boat or a ship. The bow is smooth and slim and ends in a point. This shape helps the boat to cut through the water easily.

carbon fiber
A material made of long threads of carbon, which is a very strong, black substance. The threads are covered in plastic.

cargo
Goods carried by a boat or any other vehicle.

catamaran
A boat with two hulls. A catamaran can also be called a multihull.

clipper
A fast ship with large sails. Clippers were the fastest cargo ships of the nineteenth century. They were called clippers because they "clipped," or cut, days off the time other cargo ships took to cross the ocean.

cockpit
The small space in a race boat or in any other racing vehicle where the crew sits. The cockpit is low and streamlined, and the cockpit cover is clear to give the crew a good view.

drag
Drag, or water resistance, is the force that pushes against a boat as it moves through the water. This slows the boat down.

fins
Small wings sticking out from the back of an underwater craft. The fins keep the craft steady and help to control the way it moves.

flexible
A flexible material bends easily without breaking.

heads-up display
A system that displays important information about a boat's speed and position on the windshield in front of the driver. The driver can then concentrate on steering the boat without having to look down at the controls all the time.

helm
The steering wheel and other controls. The driver stands at the helm to steer the boat.

honeycomb
The shape of a material that is specially layered and built up so that it is full of holes. This makes it thick and strong but not too heavy.

hull
The main body of a boat that sits in the water.

hydrofoil
A type of boat that has underwater wings. The wings, or foils, are attached to long stilts underneath the hull. As the boat moves, the wings lift the hull out of the water.

hydroplane
A powerboat with a specially shaped hull that lifts out of the water when the boat starts to move quickly. Hydroplanes can skim across the water at high speeds.

inflatable
Filled with air. Inflatable boats are small crafts with an air-filled rubber ring around the hull. They are used for fun and for emergency rescue work.

keel
Part of a yacht's hull that hangs down in the water. It is heavy to keep the boat from being blown over by strong winds.

knot
A measurement used to describe the speed of boats and ships. One knot equals 1.15 mph (1.85 kph).

monohull
A boat with one hull.

multihull
A boat with more than one hull. A boat with two hulls can also be called a catamaran. A boat with three hulls is also called a trimaran.

nuclear engine
This type of engine uses nuclear energy to drive it along. Nuclear power comes from a chemical reaction.

ocean liner
A large ship used to transport passengers across the ocean. Today big, comfortable liners are used for long, luxury cruises across the ocean.

paddle steamer
An old-fashioned type of ship. It has one or two large wheels with flat, wide blades. An engine powers the wheels, which turn to push the ship through the water.

patrol boat
A military boat that circles a certain area to make security checks or to keep watch on something.

pitch
To move up and down. A boat pitches up and down in a rough sea.

polyester
A thin, plastic material. It is used to make sails because it does not tear easily.

prototype
The first full-sized boat that is built using a new design. The prototype is tested to make sure that it works properly. Then many more boats are built and sold to the public or put into service.

radar
Equipment that can pick up signals from objects that are too far away to be seen, and calculate their exact position. The results are shown on a radar screen, which looks like a computer screen.

sea trial
A test carried out at sea to check that every part of a new boat is in working order.

shaft
A long pole that can be used to connect a boat propeller to the engine. The engine turns the shaft, which then turns the propeller.

shallow
Water that is not deep.

skim
To race quickly and lightly over the water, barely touching the surface.

stealth ship
A military boat that is specially designed to travel across an ocean without being seen on enemy radar screens. Stealth ships are used for secret missions or surprise attacks.

stern
The back of a boat or a ship. The stern is always much wider than the front, or the bow, of the boat.

streamlined
A smooth and slim shape. The hulls of fast boats are streamlined so that they slip through the water easily.

strut
A rod that holds part of a boat in place. Hydrofoils have long struts underneath the hull that hold the wings in place under the water.

tanker
A ship that is designed to carry large amounts of liquid, such as oil.

tow
To pull something along on a rope or a wire.

trifoiler
A boat with three hulls that are so small they are more like floats. The *Yellow Pages Endeavour* boat is the best example of a trifoiler.

turbine
Part of a jet engine. A turbine is a flat, round plate with blades around the edge. Hot gases rush through the engine and make the turbine spin around. The turbine makes the propeller turn.

wingsail boat
A new kind of boat with three sails that look like aircraft wings standing straight up. The sails are controlled by a computer on board the boat. They work much better than ordinary cloth sails.

yacht
A boat that uses sail power. Yachts are used for racing and for fun.

Index